# George Brown, CLASS CLOWN

Trouble
Magnet

GROSSET & DUNLAP
Published by the Penguin Group
Penguin Group (USA) Inc., 375 Hudson Street, New York,
New York 10014, USA
Penguin Group (Canada), 90 Eglinton Avenue East, Suite 700,
Toronto, Ontario M4P 2Y3, Canada
(a division of Pearson Penguin Canada Inc.)
Penguin Books Ltd., 80 Strand, London WC2R 0RL, England
Penguin Group Ireland, 25 St. Stephen's Green, Dublin 2, Ireland
(a division of Penguin Books Ltd.)
Penguin Group (Australia), 250 Camberwell Road, Camberwell,
Victoria 3124, Australia
(a division of Pearson Australia Group Pty. Ltd.)
Penguin Books India Pvt. Ltd., 11 Community Centre, Panchsheel Park,
New Delhi—110 017, India
Penguin Group (NZ), 67 Apollo Drive, Rosedale,
North Shore 0632, New Zealand
(a division of Pearson New Zealand Ltd.)
Penguin Books (South Africa) (Pty.) Ltd., 24 Sturdee Avenue,
Rosebank, Johannesburg 2196, South Africa

Penguin Books Ltd., Registered Offices:
80 Strand, London WC2R 0RL, England

Text copyright © 2010 Nancy Krulik. Illustrations copyright © 2010
Aaron Blecha. All rights reserved. Published by Grosset & Dunlap,
a division of Penguin Young Readers Group, 345 Hudson Street,
New York, New York 10014. GROSSET & DUNLAP is a trademark of
Penguin Group (USA) Inc. Printed in the U.S.A.

Library of Congress Control Number: 2009042078

ISBN 978-0-448-45368-2

For Danny, who loves to laugh.–NK

For Dad, thank you!–AB

# George Brown, CLASS CLOWN

## Trouble Magnet

by Nancy Krulik

illustrated by Aaron Blecha

Grosset & Dunlap

An Imprint of Penguin Group (USA) Inc.

# Chapter 1

"Okay, this is just wrong," George Brown whispered to his friend Alex. They were in the school gym, watching their fourth-grade teacher, Mrs. Kelly, do a hula dance.

"*Seriously* wrong," Alex agreed. **"Teachers shouldn't hula-hula dance."**

Mrs. Kelly gave the class **a big, gummy smile**. A little piece of green food was caught between her teeth.

"This move is called *'Ami 'Oniu,*" Mrs. Kelly said, swaying back and forth in a figure eight.

It's embarrassing when your teacher is dancing in the middle of the gym floor with a grass skirt over her pants and a paper flower necklace around her neck. But George didn't even crack a smile. He knew better. Mrs. Kelly took her dancing really seriously. It wouldn't be nice to laugh. And George was trying really hard to be a nice, well-behaved fourth-grader. **His days of being the class clown were over.**

"Hula dances tell a story," Mrs. Kelly told the class. She straightened her crooked, black glasses. "The dance I'm doing now is about catching fish in the ocean."

Mrs. Kelly moved her arms up and down like waves in the ocean. The skin on the back of her arms wiggled and jiggled as she waved. The wiggly, jiggly skin kept on waving, even after

2

Mrs. Kelly stopped moving. George knew he shouldn't stare, but he couldn't help himself. **It was too gross to ignore.**

"Oh, we're going to a Hukilau," Mrs. Kelly began to sing in a high-pitched voice. She wiggled her hips and jiggled her arms. "Huki, huki, lau . . ."

The kids all stared at their teacher. This was pretty hard to believe.

"Okay, class," Mrs. Kelly called out. "Now comes the fun part. **Make up your own hula dances.** Use your bodies to tell stories."

Nobody moved.

"Come on, it's fun," Mrs. Kelly said. "Huki, huki, hukilau."

One by one, the kids began to move around. They weren't hula dances. But they were dances that told stories. *Sort of*.

Sage began stretching her arms out like tree branches. "I'm a tree reaching toward the sun."

**George rolled his eyes.** That was really cheesy. But, of course, he didn't say that. Teachers hated when you made fun of other kids.

Louie, who thought he was the coolest kid in the fourth grade, rocked out on an **air guitar**. As he played, he made twanging noises. "Twang a lang-lang-lang."

"Rock on, Louie!" his friend Mike cheered.

"Twang! Twang!" Louie sang even louder.

Julianna swung an imaginary bat at an imaginary baseball.

"And it's outta here!"
she shouted.

George hunched over and began swinging his arms. **He was an ape looking for a banana.**

But before he really got started dancing, George felt something funny in his stomach. It was like there were hundreds of tiny bubbles bouncing around inside him. Then **strange gurgling noises** started coming from the bottom of his belly.

There was a big burp inside him. And it really wanted to come out! But there was no way George was going to let it. Not here. Not now. Because his burps were magic and caused trouble with a capital *T*.

**This burp was strong.** George could already feel it bing-bonging its way out of his belly and ping-ponging its way into his chest. He had to stop it!

George dropped down to the floor on his belly. He started wriggling up and down like a giant, slithering snake. George didn't care what he looked like. He would do anything to bump that burp back down. He pinched his nose and clamped his mouth shut.

*Stay down, burp*, George ordered. *I*

*mean it. Stay down.*

"Wow, George, look at you!" Mrs. Kelly said. "What kind of story are you trying to tell us?"

George gulped. There was definitely a story behind the dance he was doing. It just wasn't one he could tell his teacher. No way! The super burps were **George's secret**. And he was going to keep it that way.

# Chapter 2

It had all started on George's first day at Edith B. Sugarman Elementary School. George's dad was in the army, and his family moved around a lot. So here they were living in Beaver Brook, and once again George was at a new school. By now, George knew that when you're the new kid, you expect the first day to be rotten. **But *this* first day was the rottenest.**

George had promised himself to turn over a new leaf. **No more pranks.** No more class clown. He wasn't going to get into any trouble anymore, like he had at all his old schools. And at first, it had really worked. He'd raised his hand before answering questions. He didn't make faces behind teachers' backs. And when Mrs. Kelly made him be her square-dancing partner, **George hadn't made a joke**. Not even when his teacher put on a straw hat and started yodeling.

By the end of that first day, George had the exact same number of friends he'd had at the beginning of the day. **Zero.** Being the new, well-behaved George was no fun.

That night, George's parents took him out to Ernie's Ice Cream Emporium. While they were sitting outside and George was finishing his root beer float, a shooting star flashed across the sky. So George made a wish.

*I want to make kids laugh—but not get into trouble.*

The trouble was the star was gone

before George could finish the wish. So only half came true—the first half.

A minute later, George had a **funny feeling in his belly**. It was like there were hundreds of tiny **bubbles** bouncing around in there. The bubbles bounced up and down and all around. **They ping-ponged their way into his chest** and bing-bonged their way up into his throat. And then . . .

 B-U-U-U-R-P!

George let out a big burp. A *huge* burp. A SUPER burp!

The super burp was loud, and it was *magical*.

Suddenly George lost control of his arms and legs. It was like they had

minds of their own. His hands grabbed
straws and stuck them up his nose like a
walrus. His feet jumped up on the table
and **started dancing the hokey pokey**.
Everyone at Ernie's started laughing—
except his parents.

Now every time the burp came,
trouble followed. *Plenty of trouble.*
George never knew when a burp would
strike or what it would make him do.
Like juggle raw eggs in his classroom or
skateboard right into a bucket of papier-

mâché goo in the art room. Every time the burp came, George made the other kids laugh. But he also managed to make grown-ups really mad.

That was why, at the moment, George was on the floor wriggling his body up and down like a snake.

It was why he was holding his breath and almost turning blue. George wasn't trying to make fun of hula dancing. He was just trying to keep the super burp down.

**Whoosh.** Suddenly George felt a huge bubble pop inside his stomach. All the air rushed right out of him. **The fizzy feeling was gone.**

All right! George had beaten the burp! He leaped to his feet and pumped his fist in the air.

"George?" Mrs. Kelly asked again. "Please tell us what your dance is about."

**Uh-oh.** How was he going to explain this one? "Well . . . um . . . I'm a snake," George told her. "And . . . I'm excited . . . because I just swallowed a rat. Whole."

**"Ooh, gross,"** Sage said.

"Snakes do eat rats," George told her. "We learned that at my old school."

Mrs. Kelly flashed George one of her huge, gummy smiles. "You're right," she said. "Some snakes do eat rats. That was a very original hula dance, George."

George was glad his teacher had liked his dance. But he hoped he'd never have to do that—or any other belch-squelching dances—again. He hoped the super burp was gone for good.

But somehow he doubted it.

# Chapter 3

**I NEED YOU!**

SIGN UP TOMORROW!

FOR THE ANNUAL EDITH B. SUGARMAN TALENT SHOW!

George saw the sign the minute he and the other fourth-graders walked into the cafeteria at lunch time.

**"Cool,"** George said. **"A talent show."**

"I painted the poster," his friend Chris said.

"Who's the creepy-looking lady on it?" George asked.

"That's supposed to be **Edith B. Sugarman**," Chris told him. Then he asked, "So? Are you going to sign up for the talent show?"

George shrugged. "I guess."

"You're not going to skateboard again, are you, George?" Louie said really loudly, so everyone would hear.

Mike and Max, who were like Louie's shadows, started to laugh.

**George made a face.** Skateboarding in the school hallway hadn't been his fault. But of course he couldn't tell Louie that. Louie would never believe there was such a thing as a magic super burp. Who would?

"Maybe we could be superheroes," Chris suggested to George and Alex. "I could be Spiderman. Alex could be

Superman. And, George, you could be
Batman."

Chris had more superhero comic
books than anybody George had ever
known.

He was even writing
his own comic book
about a superhero
he'd made up,
Toiletman.

"What would
we *do* as superheroes?" Alex asked.
"Just stand onstage in old Halloween
costumes?"

"We could attach ourselves to wires,
and some of the other kids could pull us
up into the air," Chris told him. **"That
would be really cool."**

George wasn't so sure. What if the
wires broke? No way George wanted to
go from Batman to Splatman in front of
the whole school.

George sat down at the lunch table.
Chris and Alex sat on either side of him.

"What did your mom pack today?"
Alex asked George.

George peeked into his lunch bag. **"A baloney sandwich,"** he said. "And a banana."

"I got ham and cheese," Chris said. "And a bag of peanuts."

"I have egg salad," Alex told the boys. "Anyone want to trade?"

George and Chris shook their heads.

"I know. Egg salad is the worst," Alex admitted, sniffing his sandwich. "It kind of **smells like the bathroom** after my dad's been in there a long time."

George and Chris laughed. They knew exactly what he meant.

George looked down at his baloney sandwich. For a minute, he thought

about poking holes in two balogney slices and putting them over his face like a mask. **That would totally crack Chris and Alex up.** Chris would probably call George *Baloneyman* or something.

But as George peeled off the baloney slices, he caught a glimpse of the cafeteria lady.

**She was staring right at him.**

Cafeteria ladies definitely didn't like masks made out of baloney slices. They took food really seriously.

Besides, baloney masks were something the old George would make. The new and improved George didn't play with his food. So George closed his sandwich up again and took a bite.

"There's a game of **killer ball** going on," Alex said as he, Chris, and George went out to the school yard for recess. "You guys want to play?"

Killer ball was a game Louie had invented. It was kind of like dodgeball.

"We always lose," Chris said.

"Because we're never on Louie's team," Alex told him.

The boys watched as Louie clobbered Julianna on the back with a soccer ball.

**"Ouch!"** Julianna shouted. "You didn't have to throw it so hard."

"See?" Alex said.

Chris popped some of his peanuts into his mouth.

Just then, two chattering squirrels ran right past the boys and up a tree. George was about to suggest that they throw the squirrels a few peanuts. But before he could even open his mouth, he felt **a strange bubbling** in the bottom of his belly. Maybe it was the baloney sandwich . . . *or maybe it wasn't.*

**Oh man! Not again.**

George tried desperately to stop the bubbles. He held his nose and clamped his mouth shut.

"George, what are you doing?" Chris asked him.

George didn't answer. He was afraid to talk. **Those bubbles were strong.**

George had already kept one inside today. But this one seemed determined to get out.

The bubbles ping-pong-pinged their way up out of George's stomach.

They boing-bing-boinged their way to his chest.

They bing-boing-binged their way up his throat. And then . . .

**George let out a supersonic burp!**
It was so loud, it made the leaves on the trees shake. Kids clear across the playground could hear it.

**"Whoaaaa!"** Alex exclaimed.

**"Impressive!"** Chris added.

George opened his mouth and tried to

say, "Excuse me." But those weren't the words that came out. Instead, he said, "You know how you catch a squirrel? You climb a tree and act like a nut!"

And with that, George's feet started running toward the nearest tree. George tried to make his legs go stiff so they couldn't climb. He hugged the trunk of the tree and tried to stay on the ground. But his arms and legs had their own ideas. They wanted to climb that tree. And the next thing he knew, that's exactly what George was doing.

"**George Brown**, get down from there!" Mrs. Kelly called out. **"You'll hurt yourself."**

George wanted to get down. He really did. But his feet wouldn't let him. Up, up, up he climbed.

"Squeak! Squeak!" George chattered to a squirrel on a branch. But the

**squirrel didn't understand George's squirrel-speak**. It scampered away as fast as it could.

George's cheeks wanted to have a little squirrely fun. They sucked in a lot of air and blew themselves up like a big balloon. Now George looked like a squirrel storing nuts in his cheeks. Sort of, anyway.

"Is he trying to catch a squirrel?" George heard Chris ask.

"He's **definitely acting nutty**," Alex agreed. They were both laughing really hard.

By now the principal, Mrs. McKeon, had come out onto the playground.

"George Brown, there is **no climbing trees during recess**!" she called up to him. "You know that!"

George *did* know that. Unfortunately, the super burp didn't. And neither did his hands. They weren't about to let his cheeks have all the fun. Before George knew what was happening, his fists were drumming on his chest.

**"AHAHAHAHAHA!"** George let out a yell. He was no ordinary squirrel. He was a Tarzan squirrel.

"George!" Mrs. McKeon shouted angrily. **"Get down this minute!"**

"AHAHAHAHAHA!" George shouted even louder. His arms reached out toward a long, thin branch. His feet got ready to push off so he could swing to the next tree.

*Whoosh.* Suddenly George felt **something pop in his stomach**. It was like someone had punctured a balloon. All the air rushed out of him. The super burp was gone!

But George was still up in the tree.

George looked down at the ground. *Whoa!* **He was really high up.** He grabbed the tree trunk and held on tight.

"Get down from there right now, young man," Mrs. McKeon shouted.

"Yes, ma'am," George said. Slowly, he began to climb down the tree.

Mrs. McKeon and Mrs. Kelly were both waiting for George when he reached the ground.

"I'm so disappointed, George," Mrs. Kelly said. She straightened her glasses and wiped the **little beads of sweat** from under her nose. "You know the recess rules."

"What got into you?" Mrs. McKeon asked him.

George frowned. It wasn't what got

*into* him that made him act so crazy. It was what slipped *out* of him. **That super burp was really *ba-a-ad!***

"Um . . . I don't know, ma'am," George said. He looked down at the ground.

"I suggest you save your squirrel act for the talent show," Mrs. McKeon told him. "You know the way to my office. Now march!"

George sighed and followed the principal. Another recess sitting in the gray, metal chair that made **your butt fall asleep**. Another recess sitting listening to Mrs. McKeon's pen scratching against the papers on her desk.

Another recess staring out the window while the other kids got to play.

# Chapter 4

"I'm going to act out a scene from my comic book," Chris said as he, Alex, and George walked to school the next morning. "My mom said I can use **an old toilet plunger and a toilet seat for my sword and shield**."

"Cool," George said.

"I'm signing up to work backstage," Alex said. "I don't have any talent. At least not the kind you perform in a talent show."

George understood what his friend meant. Alex was good at math and science. But you couldn't stand up in front of an audience and do long division.

Working backstage wasn't such a bad idea. Teachers really liked when you helped out with things like that. Maybe if he did that, Mrs. Kelly might forgive him for recess yesterday.

"Maybe I'll work backstage with you," George told Alex.

**"Awesome,"** Alex said. "They need a lot of help with the curtains and the lights and stuff."

George didn't want to just work backstage. He did have some talent show talents. **He wanted to do an act, too. He just didn't know what kind. Not yet.**

All morning, George couldn't help thinking about the talent show. While the class was working on their grammar worksheets, George pictured himself singing to the crowd. Unfortunately, George wasn't a great singer. And a minute later, he pictured the crowd throwing squishy tomatoes at his head.

During math, while part of his brain was busy working on multiplication problems, the other part was thinking about a stand-up comedy routine. He knew a lot of really funny jokes like the one he e-mailed last night to his old friend Kevin back in Cherrydale: **How can you tell if an elephant's been in your refrigerator? You find his footprint in the peanut butter.**

George laughed quietly at his own joke. But apparently not quietly enough.

"George!" Mrs. Kelly scolded. "Can you tell me what's so funny about this math problem?"

**"N-n-nothing,"** George said.

"I'm going to read this poem called 'Casey at the Bat,'" Julianna said at lunch. "It's all about **this amazing baseball player**. Well, he's amazing until the end of the poem, anyway. Then he strikes out."

"Ariella, Tess, Molly, and I are rehearsing our dance after school today," Sage said. "We have the music picked out already. It's called the Four Seasons."

"What are we gonna do, Louie?" Max asked.

Louie looked at him. "We're gonna start a band and the talent show will be our first gig," he said. "I'm on guitar and Mike's on drums."

Max frowned. "I don't play anything," he said. "How am I supposed to be in the band?"

Louie thought about that for a minute. Finally he said, "You can be the roadie."

"Cool!" Max said. Then he stopped and gave Louie a confused look. "What's a roadie?" he asked.

**"A roadie is the guy who sets up equipment,"** George told him. "He also gets the sandwiches and sodas and stuff."

Louie shot George a look that said, *Who asked you?*

"I can play stuff," George told Louie, Mike, and Max. "At my old school, I learned to play tuba and . . ."

Louie burst out laughing. "Tuba?" he

asked. "Are you kidding? Whoever heard of a tuba in a rock band?"

**"Not me,"** Mike and Max said at the same time.

"Let me finish," George said. "I also play keyboard. I was in a rock band at my old school. We were **Slinky and the Worms**."

**"That's a dumb name**," Louie said.

"Look, maybe I could play keyboard for you," George told him.

Alex and Chris were looking at George

as if he were out of his mind. He could practically hear them thinking, *Why would George want to play in a band with Louie?*

George was sort of asking himself the same question. But Louie was starting a band. And even though George could have played keyboard on his own during the talent show, that wouldn't be as cool as being in a band. Besides, playing alone meant everybody in the audience could tell when you made a mistake. In a band it was much harder to figure out who was messing up.

**Louie looked at him strangely.** "Why would I want you on keyboard?" he asked.

"Because guitar and drums don't make much of a band," George explained.

It was hard for Louie to argue with that. "Well, how do I know you can play?" he asked finally.

"Yeah, you could be making this whole Slinky the Worm thing up," Max added.

"Slinky *and* the Worms," George corrected him. "And I'm not making it up."

**"Prove it,"** Louie said. "Come to my house. Then I'll decide if you're good enough to be in the band.

"Anytime you want," George replied.

Louie stood up. "Okay, I'm done eating," Louie said, pushing his tray away. "Time for some killer ball."

**"I'm done**, too," Mike said.

**"Me three,"** Max agreed.

Louie, Max, and Mike started to walk out of the cafeteria. But before they did, Louie turned around. "Oh, and one more thing," he told George. "I'm lead singer."

Suddenly, George felt a little bubble brewing up inside—kind of like he was going to burp. He opened his mouth to say, "Okay." But out came a little burp. And then he said, "You should sing solo. *So low* no one can hear you."

Chris and Alex started to laugh.

"What did you say?" Louie asked.

George didn't answer. That had been **a mini-magic burp**. The next one might be a whopper.

"He said that he thought so," Chris told Louie. "I heard him."

"Yeah, that's what I figured he said," Louie said. But he didn't sound like he really believed it.

George shot Chris **a closed-mouth smile**. But he didn't say a thing. He was afraid to open his mouth.

When Louie was gone, Chris asked, "How come you want to be in Louie's band?"

"Being in a band is cool," George said.

"Yeah, I guess," Alex agreed. "If I could play guitar, I'd be in a band."

It would have been great to be in a band with Chris and Alex. But since that wasn't going to happen, George would have to settle for being in Louie's band.

George watched through the cafeteria window. Louie really **nailed a third-grader** in killer ball.

*Gulp.* What if Louie played just as hard at killer *band*?

# Chapter 5

"Okay, class, get ready to go to the library," Mrs. Kelly announced the next morning to the kids in class 401. "We're going to do some research on your fiftieth state projects."

"Which state is the fiftieth state?" George asked. Then he covered his mouth quickly. He hadn't meant to talk without raising his hand. It had just happened. **And he couldn't even blame the burp.**

But Mrs. Kelly didn't seem angry. "I'm glad somebody asked that question, George," she said. "It's Hawaii. We're going to study all fifty states, starting with the newest one. After finishing your research on Hawaii, each of you is going to make a project and present it to the class."

"Can we work in groups?" Alex asked.

"You can work alone or in groups of no more than three people," Mrs. Kelly said. "But if you work in groups, I expect your project to be **extra special**."

"Want to work with me?" Alex whispered to George as the class lined up at the door. "I bet we come up with something really awesome."

**"Totally,"** George agreed. "We'll do a project Mrs. Kelly won't ever forget."

A few minutes later, George and Alex were seated at a table in the library looking at books about Hawaii.

"We could do a report on surfing," George said. "Did you know skateboarding was started by surfers? **It's kind of like surfing on land**."

Alex shook his head. "I don't think Mrs. Kelly would like hearing about skateboarding," he reminded George. "Not so soon after what happened."

George frowned. Alex was right. It was probably best not to remind his teacher about when he skateboarded through the halls of Edith B. Sugarman Elementary School.

"So what else can we do that's cool?" George asked. "I'm not making grass skirts or flower leis."

"And I don't ever want to **hula dance** again, either," Alex said.

**"Definitely not,"** George agreed. He turned the page in one of his books. Something caught his eye. "That's it!" he said suddenly.

"Shhh . . ." Mrs. Kelly whispered.

*Oops.* George lowered his voice immediately. "The book says Hawaii is built on volcanoes," he whispered to Alex. **"Let's make a volcano."**

"Cool!" Alex whispered back. "We can build it out of clay."

"And then we can make it erupt at the end of our presentation," George added.

"How can we do that?" Alex asked.

George shrugged. "I'm not sure. But I bet we can find directions for making **an erupting volcano**."

For the next forty-five minutes, Alex and George looked in books with science experiments until they found directions for making a fake volcano erupt.

"This is going to be so cool," Alex said. "We can build a little clay village around the volcano."

"Yeah, and when the lava spills out, it'll destroy all the buildings," George said excitedly. "Just knock them to the ground and **bury them in hot, flowing goo**."

"I have tons of old action figures we can use as villagers," Alex added.

At just that moment, Louie

and Max walked past the desk where George and Alex were sitting.

"What are you two so excited about?" Louie asked.

"Our project," Alex said. "It's going to be **amazing**."

"What are you doing?" Louie asked.

Alex opened his mouth to answer, but George stopped him.

"It's **a surprise**," George told Louie. "And there's a lot we need to do."

"Let's go to my house right after school," Alex suggested.

"Sounds like a plan," George said.

"Oh, no, it doesn't," Louie told George.

"Why not?" George asked.

"Because you're trying out for the band," Louie answered.

"Since when?" George asked.

"Since now," Louie told him. "Unless you don't want to be in the band. Today's the only day you can try out."

George looked from Alex to Louie and back again. He didn't know what to do.

"It's okay," Alex told George. "We can get started tomorrow after school."

"Be at my house at four," Louie said. "And **you'd better be as good as you say you are**. Because Mike and I are awesome."

"Hey, what about me?" Max asked Louie.

"Oh yeah," Louie said. "You make good peanut butter and jelly sandwiches."

"That's my job," Max said proudly. "I'm the roadie."

**"I like PB&J,"** George told Max.

"You don't get any sandwiches unless you make the band," Louie said to George. "And I'm the one who decides if you're in or out."

# Chapter 6

"Remember, I decide if you're in our band," Louie told George when he got to Louie's house.

"I know," George told him. **How could he *not* know?** Louie had been reminding him all day long. He almost felt like saying, "Forget it, find somebody else to be in your dumb band." But he didn't. That wouldn't be cool. And the whole point of being in a band was to be cool.

"Everything is set up in the basement," Louie told George. **"Keyboard, drums, and guitar amps, too."**

"You play all those instruments?" George asked.

Louie shook his head. "I just play guitar. My brother, Sam, plays drums and guitar. And my *mother* plays keyboard. Just like you."

Mike and Max thought that was **hilarious**. Max laughed so hard, he actually snorted.

George frowned. He knew why they were laughing. It was never cool to do something that someone's mother did.

"Come on, **let's get started**," Louie said as he began to lead the boys to the basement. He sped down one of the long hallways on the wheels in his sneakers.

Louie's house was huge! The dining room was big enough to fit their whole class for lunch!

*No wonder Louie has sneakers with wheels*, George thought. *He needs wheels to get around this place!*

As George passed the family room, he saw the walls were covered with photos. Most were of Louie and his brother on vacations— at the beach, on skis, and at amusement parks. In the living room, George spotted a **huge, flat screen TV**. Wow! It would be awesome to have one of those.

George followed Louie down the narrow stairs off the kitchen to the basement. Sure enough, there were the **drums**, the **amps**, and a small, black **keyboard**. There were also glass shelves with about a million trophies and ribbons on them.

"Are these yours?" George asked Louie.

Louie shook his head. "Uh—most of them are my brother Sam's."

"Sam's the star pitcher for the middle school baseball team," Max told George.

"And last year he won the county spelling bee," Mike added.

**"I have trophies, too,"** Louie said. "Like over there. I got that one for coming in third in a swim race at camp."

"Cool," George said.

"And this year, I'm going to win first place in the talent show," Louie said. "You get a trophy for that. Well, don't just stand there," he said. "Let's see what you can do."

George could feel **a nervous feeling** starting up in his belly. It wasn't like bouncing burp bubbles or anything. It was more like a bunch of slimy worms crawling all around inside him.

But that wasn't going to stop George from playing. He knew he was good. Now he'd show Louie. He wriggled his fingers to loosen them up. Then he started playing one of his favorites from when he was in Slinky and the Worms.

"**Bang your head**. Stomp your feet. Don't you think music's neat?" George sang as he played the keyboard.

"What song is that?" Louie asked him.

"It's called 'Bang Your Head,'" George answered.

"I've never heard of it," Louie said.

"Me neither," Max agreed.

"That's because **I wrote it**," George said. "Well, me and my friends Kevin and Jeremy. The kids in Cherrydale really liked it."

"Well, this is Beaver Brook," Louie said. "How can I tell if you're playing all the right notes if it's **a made-up song**?"

George shrugged. "I can play something else. How about 'Don't Stop Believing'?"

"My brother's band played that in their concert last year," Louie said.

George smiled proudly. He knew that Sam was in middle school. George was only in elementary school and he already knew the song. He put his fingers on the keyboard and began to play. George didn't miss a note.

When the song ended, George waited for someone to say something. But no one did. At least not at first. Then finally, **Louie frowned.**

"I guess that was okay," he said. "And besides, we need a keyboard in the band. You're in."

"Awesome," George said. And he really meant it.

**"Are you hungry?"** Max asked.

George looked over at the table in the corner where Max was making sandwiches. He watched Max smear some grape jelly and peanut butter on two slices of bread. **He wiped some snot** from his nose with his hand and then slapped the slices of bread together.

"Here," Max said.

**"Um . . . no thanks,"** George told him. "I'm not really hungry." *Anymore.*

"Okay, so now we have to come up with a name for the band," Louie said. "What do you guys think of Louie and the Lice?"

George made a face. "I don't want to be called a louse."

"Well, I like it," Louie said. "And unless you can come up with something better, that's the name."

*Snort.* George listened as Max sucked some snot back up his nose. Then he watched as he wiped his nose with the back of his hand.

**"What about the Runny Noses,"** George said quietly.

"What did you say?" Louie asked him.

"The Runny Noses," George repeated. "We could be the Runny Noses."

**"That's pretty good,"** Mike said. Then he looked quickly over at Louie. "I mean, I'm not sure. Do you like it, Louie?"

"It's actually not bad," Louie told him.

"Where'd you get that idea?" Max asked George. **"Aaachooo!"**

George laughed. "I guess it was just something I heard somewhere."

"Well, pretty soon everyone is going to hear about us," Louie said. "The Runny Noses are going to be the biggest band in **Edith B. Sugarman Elementary** history!"

"What do you mean, you don't know how to play 'Don't Drop the Rock'?" Louie shouted at George during their band rehearsal a few days later. "It's the first song you learn on guitar."

"But I don't play guitar," George told Louie. "I play piano. Do you know **'I'm Not Lazy, I'm Just Crazy'**?"

"Never heard of it," Louie said.

"Me neither," Mike said. He bashed his cymbals, and then hit one of his drums. "I want to play something with a fast beat."

"Anyone want **a salami sandwich**?" Max asked.

**"No!"** Mike, Louie, and George all shouted at once. It was the first thing the three of them had agreed on all afternoon.

"This is why my old band wrote our own songs," George told Louie and Mike. "That way we all learned the song together."

"Will you stop talking about your old band?" Louie shouted. Then he stopped for a minute. **"I know,"** he said. "Why don't we write our own song? Something no one has ever heard before. Then they won't know if we're playing right or wrong."

George was about to say that he'd just suggested that. But he knew Louie well enough not to bother.

An hour later, the Runny Noses had written their first song. Well, at least part of it, anyway.

**"Let's take it from the top,"** Louie told George and Mike. "Then maybe we can figure out what's not working."

George put his fingers on the keyboard. Mike **clicked his sticks** together.

"Five, six, seven, eight . . ." Mike said.

"What are you doing?" Louie demanded.

FIVE!
SIX!
SEVEN!
EIGHT!

"He's counting us down," George told him. "The drummer always counts to eight before the song starts. That way we all start playing at the same time. It's really important to count."

"Then I should do it," Louie said. "After all, I'm the leader of this band."

George shrugged. He didn't really care who counted. Just as long as they could play already.

"Five, six, seven, eight," Louie counted. Then the band started to play.

"We're the Runny Noses and we're running after you . . ." Louie sang.

The guys didn't get too far into the song before **Louie's big brother**, Sam, came downstairs to see what was going on.

"Yo, dude, is this your band?" Sam asked Louie.

"Yeah," Louie said. He sounded more quiet than usual.

"I never heard that song before," Sam said.

"Yeah, well, we wrote it," Louie mumbled. **He slumped a little bit**. "I know it's not great but we're . . ."

"No, it's actually pretty good," Sam told him.

Louie stood a little taller. "I wrote most of it," he boasted.

George knew **that wasn't true**. But he didn't say anything.

"But the opening chords need some work," Sam said.

"That's just what I was thinking," Louie agreed.

"Mind if I take a crack at it?" Sam asked. "Maybe I can help you guys out."

Louie shrugged, and slipped out of his guitar strap. "Sure, if you want," he said, handing Sam the guitar.

"Cool," Sam said. He swung the guitar strap over his shoulder and looked at Mike. "**Count us down**, would you, Mike?"

"Okay," Mike said. He clicked his sticks. **"Five, six, seven, eight . . ."**

Sam began to play. He was really good. Louie was good, too. But not like his brother. Sam knew exactly which chords gave the song a really strong opening riff.

Louie sat on the couch, watching as Sam led the Runny Noses through the beginning of their new song. **There was a funny expression on his face.**

Having a brother who was amazing at everything had to be tough when you were just a normal kid. Not that anyone would *ever* accuse Louie of being normal.

# Chapter 7

"Okay, this guy can go over here," Alex said. He put an action figure near the base of the volcano he and George had built. It was Saturday morning, and they were putting the finishing touches on their Hawaii project.

**"You're putting R2D2 in a Hawaiian village?"** George asked Alex. "He's a robot."

"But he's broken, so I don't care if he gets messed up," Alex said.

**"I guess** it will work," George said.

"Once the volcano erupts, you won't be able to see him or any of that village."

"That's kind of **a bummer**," Alex said. "We worked so hard on it this week."

George nodded. They had done lots of research on Mauna Loa, the largest volcano in the world. Building the volcano and village hadn't been easy, because Louie had called about a million band rehearsals. It had been a long week. But at least **George had been burp-free**.

"Erupting is what volcanoes do," George told Alex. "They explode and destroy. Kapow!"

**"Kapow!"** Alex repeated. "You're sure about how much baking soda and cherry Jell-O powder to pour into the vinegar?"

"Exactly half of this bag," George said, holding up a plastic bag filled with Jell-O powder and baking soda. "Any less and it won't explode. Any more, and we'll make a major mess."

"This is going to be so cool," Alex said. **"I can't wait until Monday morning!"**

George nodded. "When this volcano erupts, everyone is going to totally freak."

"Some leis are made from flowers. Others are made from seashells or feathers," Sage said as she gave her report to the class on Monday morning. She had a **lei around her neck**.

"When someone gives you a lei, it is supposed to show that they like you."

George put his hand over his mouth and tried to hide a yawn. Sage's report was boring. Louie's report on ukuleles hadn't been much better.

In fact, so far, the

only report that had been even *kind of* cool was Julianna's about poi. **Poi was this soupy, pudding-y mush** that was made of the root of some plant. Julianna had made enough for everyone to try. And the way you ate it was by scooping it up with your fingers. It didn't taste bad for something that looked pretty nasty.

George thought the poi looked a little like the **"George soup"** he used to make during lunchtime at his old school—especially the kind where he mixed up fruit punch, vanilla pudding, and salad dressing. When he was really goofing off, he used to stick some of his action figures in the George soup and pretend they were stuck in quicksand. *Good times.*

Today, those same action figures were *really* going to get it. Just as soon as the volcano exploded!

Finally, it was George and Alex's turn. They carried their volcano to the front of the room. George placed it on the table and stood back. Then he reached into his pocket and pulled out the container of **secret erupting powder**. At the end of Alex's report on the **Mauna Loa volcano**, George was going to pour half of the powder into the bottle of vinegar that was hidden inside the volcano, and make it erupt.

"The Hawaiian islands were all created by volcanoes," Alex said. "They started from

hot spots deep in the earth. A stream of superhot rock, called lava, was forced up from the hot spot. This caused volcanoes to form."

George stood there quietly, listening to Alex speak. Suddenly, he felt something **weird** in the bottom of his belly. It was a fizzy feeling. Like a million soda bubbles were bouncing around in there.

**Oh no! Not the super burp!** He'd been burp-less for a week! How could this be happening now?

"This volcano is called Mauna Loa, which means Long Mountain in Hawaiian," Alex read from his paper. "It's the largest volcano on our planet . . ."

**George couldn't pay attention** to what Alex was saying. He couldn't pay attention to anything but the burp swelling inside him—the super burp. It was back, and it wanted to come out. Already the bubbles were bing-bonging in George's belly, and ping-ponging their way up into his chest.

"Mauna Loa has erupted thirty-nine times since 1832," Alex continued. "Its most recent eruption was in 1984. And scientists say it is sure to erupt again . . ."

George had to stop that burp. He just had to. **He shut his lips tight and held his nose.** Then he swallowed really hard, trying to force the burp back down his throat.

But the super burp was strong. It had been kept down for too long. It needed to break free.

The biggest burp in the world erupted. **A supercolossal, Mauna Loa-size burp.** A burp so loud, it could probably be heard all the way across the Pacific Ocean in Hawaii!

Alex stopped talking and stared at George. The kids all started laughing. Mrs. Kelly stood up.

"Quiet, class," she said. "I'm sure George didn't mean to do that."

**That was sure the truth.**

George opened his mouth to say, "Excuse me." But nothing came out. Instead, his hands started moving. It was like they had a mind of their own. They popped off the top of the container they had been holding. There was no way to stop them from pouring *all* of the secret erupting powder into the vinegar.

**"George!"** Alex shouted. "What are you doing? You're only supposed to put in half of the powd—"

Alex never finished his sentence.

The volcano began to shake. It began to tremor. And then . . .

**KAPOW!** The volcano erupted. Ruby red "lava" gel shot way up in the air!

Now George's feet wanted to have some fun. They began to leap up and down like they were on fiery coals.

**"Hot! Hot!"** George's mouth shouted out. **"Hot lava!"**

George began to roll on the floor under the shower of vinegar, Jell-O, and

baking soda lava. "Oh no! **I'm being buried by lava**!" he shouted.

"George! What are you doing?" Mrs. Kelly scolded. She pulled a tissue out from her sleeve, and wiped **lava splatters** from her glasses. "This is a science project, not the talent show."

But **George couldn't stop himself**. He wasn't in charge of his own body. The super burp was. And the super burp wanted George to roll around on the floor.

"Hot lava!" he shouted. "Help!"

*Whoosh!* Suddenly, George felt something pop in his belly. It was kind of like a balloon being punctured with a needle. All the air rushed right out of him. **The super burp was gone.**

But George was still there. In front of the classroom. On the floor. With red lava

all over the place. He opened his mouth to say, "I'm sorry." And those were exactly the words that came out.

**"What were you thinking?"** Mrs. Kelly asked.

She didn't sound angry. She sounded disappointed. That was worse.

George knew he'd better not say that he *wasn't* thinking. That was the kind of answer that could get a kid in even more trouble. So instead, he said, "I guess I was trying to show how sometimes volcanoes can erupt without warning. I didn't mean to mess up the classroom." **That was the truth.** He hadn't.

Mrs. Kelly sighed. "It's true that volcanoes can erupt suddenly. But I don't think what you did was the best way to demonstrate that."

"**I'm really sorry**, Mrs. Kelly," George said. He looked down at the gooey, red mess in front of him.

Mrs. Kelly looked puzzled and shook her head. "That's a start," she told him. "Shouldn't you also tell Alex you're sorry? After all, he worked hard on this project."

"I'm really sorry, dude," George said to Alex. **"I didn't mean to ruin everything."**

Alex didn't answer. George could tell he was really mad. Nothing George could say or do was going to make this better right now.

Sadly, George looked up at Mrs. Kelly. "I guess I'll go find Mr. Coleman and get a mop," he told his teacher.

"It's going to take a while to clean up this mess." Mrs. Kelly shook her head again. "I honestly don't know why you do these things, George."

George knew why. But he didn't know why the super burp picked him of all kids in the world as the victim. **It wasn't fair. Not at all.**

George skateboarded home from band rehearsal later that day. He was really lonely. Even people on the street seemed to move far away from him. Of course that was probably because they didn't want him to crash into them. Or maybe because **he smelled nasty**—like old salad dressing, from the vinegar and Jell-O that had been in his hair.

As George turned the corner and skateboarded onto his block, he spotted Chris and Alex tossing a ball around on Alex's front lawn. George could tell they

both saw him. He could also tell from Alex's face that he didn't want anything to do with George right now.

**"Yo, George,"** Chris called out. "Want to throw a ball around with us?"

George looked over at Alex. "Okay with you?" he asked.

Alex just shrugged. **"Whatever."**

"I really am sorry about today," he said. It was about the tenth time he'd said it.

"You said you knew how much stuff to put in. And why didn't you wait until I was done talking?" Alex wanted to know. "That was the plan. You were supposed to surprise everyone else but not *me*."

George wanted to say that he was just as surprised as Alex. But that would sound ridiculous. So instead he just said, "It was just **something that came over me**."

Now Alex laughed. "It came over you, all right." He was looking at the big, red stains on George's T-shirt. "*All* over you."

"Oh yeah," George agreed. **"My mom's going to freak."**

Chris held up the baseball. "You want to practice some killer ball moves? Maybe we can finally beat Louie's team."

"Sure," George said. "I'll be 'it' and try to tag you with the ball." He stopped for a minute. "**I mean if that's okay** with you guys."

"It's cool," Alex said. "I'll be 'it' after you."

"And then me," Chris agreed.

"We're definitely getting better at this game," Alex said as he started to run away from the ball.

"Yeah, we are," George agreed. And now that he and Alex were talking again, he was *feeling* a lot better, too.

# Chapter 8

For the next week, the burps only came after George left school. One came right when he was getting ready for bed, one in the storage room of his mom's craft store, and one while he was in the shower. That wasn't so bad. **At least there hadn't been any burping at school.** Which was good, because George had to spend a lot of extra time at school after classes, learning how to work the curtains in the auditorium.

George had signed up to work backstage during the talent show. He was in charge of the curtains. But when the Runny Noses went onstage, Alex was going to take over pulling the curtains. So all week long, he and Alex had spent a lot of time with Mrs. Kelly. She showed them how to work the stage lights and pull the thick cords that lifted and lowered the stage curtains between acts. It wasn't as easy as it looked. George was taking it very seriously. There was no room for joking around backstage.

**"Okay, who's next?"** Mrs. Kelly asked Alex, as the backstage crew got ready for the next act to go onstage on the night of the talent show.

Alex looked at his clipboard. "Chris."

**"It's *my* turn already?"** Chris asked. His face was ghost white. "I can't do it. **I'm too scared**."

"What do you mean?" George asked him. "You've been practicing for two weeks. And your **Toiletman** costume looks great. Your mom even bought you a new plunger!"

"What if nobody likes my jokes?" Chris said.

"They'll like them," George told him.

"Toiletman's funny," Alex agreed.

"But you guys are my friends," Chris said. "There are **a whole bunch of people** out there I don't know."

George thought for a minute. Then he said, "They're people just like us. They put their **underwear** on one leg at a time."

Chris stared at him.

"My dad said something like that to my mom when she had to make a speech to the PTA in my old school," George explained. "The point is, if you picture the people in the **audience in their underwear**, they won't seem so scary."

Chris started to laugh.

"What's so funny?" Alex asked him.

"I'm picturing Mr. Trainer in **tighty-whities**," Chris said.

Mr. Trainer was their gym teacher.

"See?" George told Chris. "It's working already."

Chris picked up his **toilet seat shield**, **his plunger**, **his toilet brush**, and a roll of toilet paper. "Toiletman will not be flushed," he said. "The show must go on."

George began to open the curtains.
**"Go, Toiletman.** I know you'll *bowl* them over!"

Once the clapping for Chris stopped, George brought down the curtains. It was time for Sage and her friends to do their dance. The girls were all dressed in different colored leotards and tights. They were each supposed to be one of the four seasons.

Up went the curtain again. George watched the girls wave their arms around and leap across the floor. **It was boring**, but watching was part of a curtain guy's job. As soon as the dance was over, he had to pull on the ropes and close the curtains.

So George watched as Sage jumped up high in her autumn costume, and bashed Ariella in the nose. Nobody stopped dancing even though **Ariella's nose was bleeding all over the place**. Wow. This was getting to be sort of entertaining, after all.

Then, right in the middle of the bloody ballet, George suddenly felt something weird happening in the bottom of his belly. There was a bubble in there. **A *big* bubble.** And it was starting to jump around.

Oh no! Not the super burp. ***Not now.***

The bubbles were already **ping-ponging** around in his stomach and threatening to move up into his chest. George gulped. **This couldn't happen.** Not in the middle of the talent show. There was no telling what his hands and feet would do if they got control of the curtains. Or worse, what if the super burp made him go out there and leap around with Sage and her friends?!

George had to **beat the burp**! Quickly, he shoved his whole fist in his mouth. There was no way the burp was getting past *that*!

But the burp was strong. And it was determined. It kept bouncing and bouncing around. George used his free hand to pound his stomach, trying to pop that bubble from the outside.

At just that moment, Louie, Max, and Mike walked over.

"Yo, what is the matter with you?" Louie asked him.

George didn't answer. He couldn't. He had his fist shoved in his mouth.

Then, suddenly, George felt something go **pop** inside. *Whoosh!* It felt like all the air rushed right out of him. **Yahoo! George had done it!** He'd squelched the belch!

George took his hand out of his mouth. He wiped his wet, **spit-covered** fingers on his jeans.

"Why were you sucking on your fingers?" Louie asked. "It's gross."

"*Really* gross," Max agreed.

"Um, it's called **a vocal exercise**," George said quickly. "You have to try and sing through your hand, while tapping on your belly." There. That sounded believable. Sort of.

"Yeah, well, don't do it again," Louie said. "You look **weird**. And I don't want anyone thinking the Runny Noses are weird."

**"No problem,"** George said.

Just then, Alex came running over. He grabbed hold of the ropes and began lowering the curtains as Sage and her friends ran offstage. It was his turn to be the curtain guy.

"Are you guys ready?" Alex asked the Runny Noses.

George sure hoped so.

# Chapter 9

"We're the Runny Noses, and we're running after you. We're the Runny Noses, can't be stopped with no tissue . . ."

George sang the background vocals as he played his keyboard. He looked into the audience to see if he could spot his parents. There were a lot of people out there, but it was *always* easy to find his dad. An army uniform really stood out in a crowd.

**"Coming to you as hard as a sneeze**. We'll play just as long as we please . . ."

The lyrics were **pretty dumb**. Louie had written them, and Mike and Max kept saying how cool the song was. So those were the words they used.

George tried to play in time with Mike's drums. **It wasn't easy.** Every now and then, Mike would speed up or slow down. But then again, George didn't always play the right notes. And Louie had forgotten a couple of words in the first verse. But no one seemed to notice. In fact, some people were clapping along.

George was starting to have a good time. Then, **suddenly**, he got a strange feeling in his stomach. A bunch of bubbles were suddenly bouncing up and down and all around in his belly.

**Oh no! Not again!**

George had to stop that burp right now! But this time he couldn't use his hands to beat down the burp. He had to keep playing.

So he just held his breath until his face turned red.

Louie turned around to face George. **"What are you doing?"** he whispered angrily.

George didn't answer. He couldn't.

The bubbles ping-pong-pinged their way up out of George's stomach.

They **boing-bing-boinged** their way to his chest.

They bing-boing-binged their way up his throat. And then . . .

George let out the loudest burp in the history of Edith B. Sugarman Elementary School. In fact, if burping counted as a talent, George would have walked away with a trophy. The super-duper **mega-burping trophy**!

The audience laughed really hard. Louie and Mike just stared at him.

"It wasn't me," George said.

The words slipped right out of George's mouth. He hadn't meant to say them.

The audience just laughed harder.

And then George's feet got a great idea! They slipped right out of their shoes and **wriggled out of his socks**. Then his feet propped themselves up on the keyboard.

George tried to stop them. He tried to slap them down from the piano.

"Stop!" he ordered.

But George's feet would not obey. His toes wanted to play the keyboard. *Go tell Aunt Rhodie. Go tell Aunt Rhodie . . .*

"What are you playing?" Louie asked. **"That's for kindergartners!"**

But it was the only song George's toes knew. So they kept playing it.

*Go tell Aunt Rhodie. Go tell Aunt Rhodie . . . Go tell Aunt Rhodie, the old gray goose is dead.*

"Cut it out!" Louie shouted.

George turned and smiled at the audience. He stood up and took a bow. **The kids all cheered wildly.**

And then, before George even knew what he was doing . . .

**"Dive-bomb!"** George shouted as he took a flying leap off the stage.

*Wahoo!* George was soaring in the air, and heading right for the crowd.

A bunch of older kids—one of them was Louie's brother—reached up. Two kids caught his legs. Someone's dad caught him right in the armpits. His head fell into someone's arms.

The crowd cheered wildly. **"George! George! George!"**

*Pop!* Just then, George felt something burst in his belly. *Whoosh.* All the air rushed right out of him.

The super burp was gone. But George was still there. As he looked up, he realized Mrs. McKeon was holding his head. And she did not look happy.

*Uh-oh.* George had just **dive-bombed into the principal**. This was *ba-a-ad!*

# Chapter 10

"**I can't believe** we didn't even come in third," Mike complained as he packed up his drumsticks after the talent show.

"Are you kidding?" Louie asked. "After what he did, we're lucky we didn't get thrown out of school."

George looked down at the ground. He felt **really bad**. Louie had wanted a trophy. They all did. And maybe they would have gotten one, except for the stupid super burp.

"We never should have let you in the band," Louie told George. **"You messed the whole thing up.** If I was Mrs. McKeon, I'd take away your recess for a whole year."

George couldn't imagine what Louie would be like as principal of a school. It was **too scary** to think about.

"You're going to be sorry you did this to me . . . I mean to *us*," Louie said. **"You're out of the band!"**

Just then, Sam and two other middle-school kids came backstage.

They were heading toward the band. *Uh-oh*. The last thing George wanted now was some older kids making fun of him.

Louie looked kind of nervous as his brother walked closer and closer. "You guys were good!" Sam said.

**"Really, Sam?** You really thought—" Louie said.

Sam didn't answer. Instead he was looking at George. "And you! You were **amazing, dude**," he told George.

**"Playing keyboard with your toes!"** Sam's friend added. "How do you do that?"

"The **dive-bomb** was the best part," Sam said.

"You guys were ripped off," the third middle-schooler told them. "You should have won."

George just stood there, surprised. He wasn't sure what to say.

"That dive-bomb was my idea," Louie told Sam. "I would have done it myself, but I didn't want to break my guitar."

George shook his head. Louie was **unbelievable**.

"At our next concert, *I'm* going to

dive-bomb," Louie told George.

Huh? **Their next concert?** What next concert? Hadn't Louie just thrown him out of the band?

Just then, Alex came over. "My mom said you and your parents should come for ice cream with us," he said to George. "We're going to Ernie's Ice Cream Emporium."

Ernie's. That was the last place George wanted to go tonight. That was where it had all started. It was the **scene of the first burp**. And George had had enough burping for one night.

**"I better not,"** George told Alex. "My parents will be waiting for me out in the hall. I have a feeling they're not going to want me to go anywhere. They're probably going to want to *talk*."

Alex nodded and then shook his head sadly. When parents wanted to talk, **it was never a good thing**.

"Well, let's hang out tomorrow if you're allowed," Alex told him. **"I'm still working on how to ollie."**

Louie shook his head. "George can't skateboard tomorrow. He's got band practice."

"Sorry, Louie. **It's not happening**," George told him. "I'm hanging out with

Alex tomorrow."

Louie stared at George, like he couldn't believe anyone would turn down a chance to hang out with him.

"We can rehearse on Sunday, though," George said.

Louie didn't look happy. But all he said was, "Okay, Sunday. Cool."

Suddenly, George heard a loud, grumbly, rumbly noise. It was coming from his stomach!

Everyone just stopped and stared.

**"Dude, gross,"** the fifth-grader said.

A familiar feeling came over George. He put his hand on his stomach. And then . . . he smiled. There was no burp in there. In fact there was *nothing* in there. His stomach was just empty.

"I'm **starving**. My stomach always grumbles when I'm hungry," George explained.

George was **happy to be burp-free—** at least for now. But somehow he had a feeling the super burp would be back. He just didn't know when. Or what it would make him do. The only thing he knew for sure was that when that burp came back, it was going to cause trouble. And that was just plain *ba-a-ad*!

# About the Author

Nancy Krulik is the author of more than 150 books for children and young adults including three *New York Times* best sellers and the popular Katie Kazoo, Switcheroo books. She lives in New York City with her family, and many of George Brown's escapades are based on things her own kids have done. (No one delivers a good burp quite like Nancy's son, Ian!) Nancy's favorite thing to do is laugh, which comes in pretty handy when you're trying to write funny books!

# About the Illustrator

Aaron Blecha was raised by a school of giant squid in Wisconsin and now lives with his wife in London, England. He works as an artist and animator designing toys, making cartoons, and illustrating books, including the Zombiekins series. You can enjoy more of his weird creations at www.monstersquid.com.